A
Child's Treasury of

SEASIDE VERSE

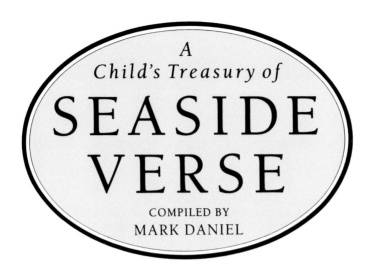

A
Child's Treasury of
SEASIDE VERSE

COMPILED BY
MARK DANIEL

Dial Books for Young Readers  New York

Published by Dial Books for Young Readers
A Division of Penguin Books USA Inc.
375 Hudson Street
New York, New York 10014
Conceived and produced by Breslich & Foss, London
Copyright © 1991 by Breslich & Foss

Printed in Hong Kong
Designed by Roger Daniels
1 3 5 7 9 10 8 6 4 2

Library of Congress Cataloging in Publication Data
A child's treasury of seaside verse
compiled by Mark Daniel.
p. cm.
Summary: A collection of verses about the sea from Byron,
Shakespeare, Whitman, and other British and American writers
of the nineteenth and early twentieth century.
ISBN 0-8037-0889-0
1. Sea poetry, English. 2. Sea poetry, American. 3. Children's
poetry, English. 4. Children's poetry, American. [1. Sea poetry.
2. English poetry—Collections. 3. American poetry—Collections.]
I. Daniel, Mark.
PR1195.S417C45 1991 821.008′032162—dc20 90-2819 CIP AC

CONTENTS

AT THE SEASIDE

6

SHIPS AT SEA

30

THE DEEP

60

OLD SALTS

82

SEA DREAMS

106

The Poets

132

The Painters

136

Acknowledgments

136

Index of First Lines

137

AT THE
SEASIDE

SEA SONG

To sea! to sea! the calm is o'er
The wanton water leaps in sport,
And rattles down the pebbly shore,
The dolphin wheels, the sea cows snort,
And unseen mermaid's pearly song
Comes bubbling up, the weeds among.
Fling broad the sail, dip deep the oar:
To sea! to sea! the calm is o'er.

To sea! to sea! our white winged bark
Shall billowing cleave its watery way,
And with its shadow, fleet and dark,
Break the caved Tritons' azure day,
Like mountain eagle soaring light
O'er antelopes on Alpine height.
The anchor heaves! the ship swings free!
Our sails swell full! To sea! to sea!

THOMAS LOVELL BEDDOES

ABOVE THE DOCK

Above the quiet dock at midnight,
Tangled in the tall mast's corded height,
Hangs the moon. What seemed so far away
Is but a child's balloon, forgotten after play.

T. E. HULME
Complete Poetical Works, 1912

THE CLIFF-TOP

The cliff-top has a carpet
  Of lilac, gold and green:
The blue sky bounds the ocean,
  The white clouds scud between.

A flock of gulls are wheeling
  And wailing round my seat;
Above my head the heaven,
  The sea beneath my feet.

ROBERT BRIDGES
The Gypsy Trail, 1930

ON THE BEACH

Gathering up the pebbles,
   Delving in the sand,
Building mimic castles,
   Wading hand in hand
With one's little neighbours —
   Happy smiles for each;
Ah! 'tis surely pleasant
   Playing on the beach.

Dimpled feet swift treading
   The huge billow's track,
Rosy fingers flinging
   Merry kisses back;
Little people striving
   First the shore to reach;
Ah! 'tis very pleasant
   Playing on the beach.

ANON

When I was down beside the sea
A wooden spade they gave to me
To dig the sandy shore.
My holes were empty like a cup,
In every hole the sea came up,
Till it could come no more.

ROBERT LOUIS STEVENSON

SHELL SECRETS

Tell me your secrets, pretty shell,
I will promise not to tell!

Humming, humming, soft and low —
All about the sea, I know.

You are murmuring, I think,
Of the sea-weeds, green and pink,

Of the tiny baby shells
Where the mother mermaid dwells,

Pretty shell, I'm waiting here,
Come and whisper in my ear.

ANON

EVENING ON THE BEACH

It is a beauteous evening, calm and free;
The holy time is quiet as a nun
Breathless with adoration; the broad sun
Is sinking down in its tranquility;
The gentleness of heaven is on the sea:
Listen! the mighty Being is awake,
And doth with his eternal motion make
A sound like thunder — everlastingly.
Dear child! dear girl! that walkest with me here,
If thou appear untouched by solemn thought
Thy nature is not therefore less divine:
Thou liest in Abraham's bosom all the year,
And worshipp'st at the Temple's inner shrine,
God being with thee when we know it not.

WILLIAM WORDSWORTH
Poems, 1807

THE SEAGULL

Oh the white seagull, the wild seagull,
  A joyful bird is he,
As he lies like a cradled thing at rest
  In the arms of a sunny sea!
The little waves rock to and fro,
  And the white gull lies asleep,
As the fishers bark, with breeze and tide,
  Goes merrily over the deep.
The ship, with her fair sails set, goes by,
  And her people stand to note
How the seagull sits on the rocking waves
  As if in an anchored boat.

The sea is fresh, the sea is fair,
  And the sky calm overhead,
And the seagull lies on the deep, deep sea,
  Like a king in his royal bed.
Oh the white seagull, the bold seagull,
  A joyful bird is he,
Throned like a king in calm repose
  On the breast of the heaving sea!

MARY HOWITT
excerpt, Birds and Flowers, 1838

THE TIDE RISES, THE TIDE FALLS

The tide rises, the tide falls,
The twilight darkens, the curlew calls;
Along the sea-sands damp and brown
The traveller hastens toward the town;
   And the tide rises, the tide falls.

Darkness settles on roofs and walls,
But the sea in the darkness calls and calls;
The little waves, with their soft white hands,
Efface the footprints in the sands,
   And the tide rises, the tide falls.

The morning breaks; the steeds in their stalls
Stamp and neigh, as the hostler calls;
The day returns; but nevermore
Returns the traveller to the shore,
   And the tide rises, the tide falls.

HENRY WADSWORTH LONGFELLOW
Complete Poetical Works, 1911

Dance to your daddy,
My little babby,
Dance to your daddy, my little lamb;
You shall have a fishy
In a little dishy,
You shall have a fishy
    when the boat comes in.

ANON

Granny and I with dear Dadu
Went rambling on the shore;
With pebbles smooth and cockleshells
We filled his pinafore.

Beneath the stones and in the pool
We found to our delight,
Shrimps, periwinkles, and a most
Voracious appetite.

D'ARCY WENTWORTH THOMPSON
Nursery Nonsense, 1864

A GOOD PLAY

We built a ship upon the stairs
All made of the back-bedroom chairs,
And filled it full of sofa pillows
To go a-sailing on the billows.

We took a saw and several nails,
And water in the nursery pails;
And Tom said, "Let us also take
An apple and a slice of cake;" —
Which was enough for Tom and me
To go a-sailing on, till tea.

We sailed along for days and days,
And had the very best of plays;
But Tom fell out and hurt his knee,
So there was no one left but me.

ROBERT LOUIS STEVENSON
A Child's Garden of Verses, 1885

MINNIE AND WINNIE

Minnie and Winnie
  Slept in a shell.
Sleep little ladies!
  And they slept well.

Pink was the shell within,
  Silver without;
Sounds of the great sea
  Wandered about.

Sleep, little ladies,
  Wake not soon!
Echo on echo
  Dies to the moon.

Two bright stars
  Peeped into the shell
"What are they dreaming of?
  Who can tell?"

Started a green linnet
  Out of the croft;
Wake, little ladies,
  The sun is aloft!

ALFRED, LORD TENNYSON
St. Nicholas, February 1880

Hey, dorolot, dorolot!
Hey, dorolay, dorolay!
Hey, my bonny boat, bonny boat,
Hey, drag away, drag away!

ANON

SEAWEED

Last summer time I went to Dover by the
sea,
And thought I'd like to bring a bunch of
seaweed home with me.
It tells you if it's going to rain, or if it's going
to snow.
And with it anyone can tell just what he
wants to know.

FRED EARLE
The Music Hall Songster, 1901

A sailor went to sea
To see what he could see
And all that he could see
Was sea, sea, sea.

ANON

I STARTED EARLY,
TOOK MY DOG

I started early, took my dog,
And visited the sea.
The mermaids in the basement
Came out to look at me.

And frigates in the upper floor
Extended hempen hands,
Presuming me to be a maise
Aground upon the sands.

But no man moved me till the tide
Went past my simple shoe
And past my apron and my belt
And past my bodice too

And made as he would eat me up
As wholly as a dew
Upon a dandelion's sleeve;
And then I started too

And he, he followed close behind;
I felt his silver heel
Upon my ankle, then my shoes
Would overflow with pearl,

Until we met the solid town.
No one he seemed to know
And bowing with a mighty look
At me, the sea withdrew.

EMILY DICKINSON
Complete Poems, 1924

SHIPS
AT SEA

A MAN-O'-WAR

He that has sail'd upon the dark blue sea,
Has viewed at times, I ween, a full fair sight;
When the fresh breeze is fair as breeze may be,
The white sails set, the gallant frigate tight,
Masts, spires, and strand retiring to the right,
The glorious main expanding o'er the bow,
The convoy spread like wild swans in their flight,
The dullest sailor wearing bravely now,
So gaily curl the waves before each dashing prow.

LORD BYRON
excerpt, Childe Harold's Pilgrimage, 1812

MY BRIGANTINE

My brigantine!
Just in thy mould and beauteous in thy form,
Gentle in roll and buoyant on the surge,
Light as the sea-fowl rocking in the storm,
In breeze and gale thy onward course we urge,
    My water-queen!

Lady of mine!
More light and swift than thou none thread the sea,
With surer keel or steadier on its path;
We brave each waste of ocean-mystery
And laugh to hear the howling tempest's wrath,
    For we are thine!

My brigantine!
Trust to the mystic power that points thy way,
Trust to the eye that pierces from afar,
Trust the red meteors that around thee play,
And, fearless, trust the Sea-Green Lady's Star,
    Thou bark divine!

JAMES FENIMORE COOPER

O'ER THE RIPPLING OCEAN

O'er the rippling ocean
  Swift the good ship flies,
With a graceful motion
  On her way she hies.

See her white sails gleaming,
  So gaily all outspread;
See her pennon streaming
  From the tall mast-head.

Sunny skies are o'er her,
  Skies of brightest blue;
And her path before her
  Smooth and tranquil too.

Prosperous gales attend thee,
  Good ship, o'er the main;
Prosperous breezes send thee
  Safely home again.

ANON

WHERE LIES
THE LAND

Where lies the land to which the ship would go?
Far, far ahead is all her seamen know.
And where the land she travels from? Away,
Far, far behind, is all that they can say.

On sunny noons upon the deck's smooth face,
Linked arm in arm, how pleasant here to pace!
Or, o'er the stern reclining, watch below
The foaming wake far-widening as we go.

On stormy nights when wild north-westerns rave,
How proud a thing to fight with wind and wave!
The dripping sailor on the reeling mast
Exults to bear, and scorns to wish it past.

Where lies the land to which the ship would go?
Far, far ahead is all her seamen know.
And where the land she travels from? Away,
Far, far behind is all that they can say.

ARTHUR HUGH CLOUGH
Poems, 1862

BOAT SONG

Lightly row, lightly row!
O'er the glassy waves we go;
Smoothly glide, smoothly glide
On the silent tide.
Let the wind and waters be
Mingled with our melody;
Sing and float, sing and float,
In our little boat.

Far away, far away!
Echo in the rocks at play
Calleth not, calleth not
To this lonely spot:
Only with the sea-birds note
Shall our dying music float;
Lightly row, lightly row!
Echo's voice is low.

Happy we, full of glee,
Sailing on the waxy sea,
Happy we, full of glee,
Sailing on the sea.
Luna sheds her softest light
Stars are sparkling, twinkling bright;
Happy we, full of glee,
Sailing on the sea.

ANON

OLD SHIP RIGGERS

Yes, we did a heap o' riggin'
In those rampin' boomin' days,
When the wooden ships were buildin'
On their quaint old greasy ways;
Crafts of every sort an' fashion,
Big an' little, lithe an' tall,
Had their birthplace by the harbour,
An' we rigged 'em one and all.

Jacob's ladder wasn't in it
With the riggin' on those ships
From the trunnels and the keelson
To the pointed royal tips;
That old ladder was for angels
Comin' down from up aloft,
With their wings an' gleamin' garments,
An' their hands all white an' soft.

Our riggin' was for sailors,
Tough an' hardy Bluenose dogs,
With their hands as hard as leather,
An' their boots thick heavy clogs,
They were nuthin' much like angels,
But they'd learned their business right,
An' they trusted to our riggin'
When the sea was roarin' white.

But our riggin' days are over,
An' the past seems like a dream,
As we view the mighty changes
Brought about by wizard steam.
We are needed here no longer
For there's nuthin' we can do —
Maybe there'll be work for riggers,
In the Port, beyond the blue.

H. A. CODY
excerpt, Song of a Bluenose, circa 1920

THE GALLANT SHIP

Upon the gale she stooped her side,
And bounded o'er the swelling tide,
   As she were dancing home;
The merry seamen laughed to see
Their gallant ship so lustily
   Furrow the sea-green foam.

SIR WALTER SCOTT

O to sail in a ship!
To leave this steady unendurable land,
To leave the tiresome sameness of the
    streets, the sidewalks and the houses,
To leave you O you solid motionless land,
    and entering a ship,
To sail and sail and sail!

WALT WHITMAN
Leaves of Grass, Book XI:
A Song of Joys, 1891 – 2

WITH SHIPS THE SEA WAS SPRINKLED FAR AND NIGH

With ships the sea was sprinkled far and nigh,
Like stars in heaven, and joyously it showed;
Some lying fast at anchor in the road,
Some veering up and down, one knew not why.
A goodly Vessel did I then espy
Come like a giant from a haven broad;
And lustily along the bay She strode,
Her tackling rich, and of apparel high.
This Ship was nought to me, nor I to her,
Yet I pursued her with a Lover's look;
This Ship to all the rest did I prefer:
When will She turn, and whither? She will brook
No tarrying; where She comes the winds must stir;
On went She, and due north her journey took.

WILLIAM WORDSWORTH
Poems, 1807

PADDLER'S SONG

Ho! merrily ho! we paddlers sail!
Ho! over sea-dingle, and dale!
All fire-flies flame with golden gleamings!
   Our pulses fly;
   Our hearts beat high,
Ho! merrily, merrily, ho!

HERMAN MELVILLE

FIFTY NORTH AND FORTY WEST

When the cabin port-holes are dark and green
   Because of the seas outside;
When the ship goes WOP (with a wiggle between)
And the steward falls in the soup-tureen,
   And the trunks begin to slide;
When Nursey lies on the floor in a heap,
And Mummy tells you to let her sleep,
And you aren't waked or washed or dressed,
Why, then you will know (if you haven't guessed)
You're Fifty North and Forty West.

RUDYARD KIPLING
Puck of Pook's Hill, 1902

THE FIGHTING TÉMÉRAIRE

It was eight bells ringing,
  For the morning watch was done,
And the gunner's lads were singing
  As they polished every gun.
It was eight bells ringing,
And the gunner's lads were singing,
For the ship she rode a-swinging
  As they polished every gun.

It was noontide ringing,
  And the battle just begun,
When the ship her way was winging
  As they loaded every gun.
It was noontide ringing,
When the ship her way was winging,
And the gunner's lads were singing
  As they loaded every gun.

There'll be many grim and gory,
  Téméraire! Téméraire!
There'll be few to tell the story,
  Téméraire! Téméraire!
There'll be many grim and gory
There'll be few to tell the story,
But we'll all be one in glory
  With the Fighting Téméraire.

Now the sunset breezes shiver,
  Téméraire! Téméraire!
And she's fading down the river,
  Téméraire! Téméraire!
Now the sunset breezes shiver
And she's fading down the river,
But in England's song for ever
  She's the Fighting Téméraire.

SIR HENRY NEWBOLT
excerpt, Admirals All and Other Verses, 1897

LANDING OF THE PILGRIM FATHERS

The breaking waves dashed high,
   On a stern and rock-bound coast,
And the woods against a stormy sky,
   Their giant branches tossed;

And the heavy night hung dark,
   The hills and waters o'er,
When a band of exiles moored their bark
   On the wild New England shore.

Not as the conqueror comes,
   They, the true-hearted came;
Not with the roll of the stirring drums,
   And the trumpet that sings of fame;

Not as the flying come,
   In silence and in fear; —
They shook the depths of the desert gloom
   With their hymns of lofty cheer.

Amidst the storm they sang,
   And the stars heard, and the sea;
And the sounding aisles of the dim woods rang
   To the anthem of the free.

Aye, call it holy ground,
   The soil where first they trod;
They have left unstained what there they found —
   Freedom to worship God.

FELICIA HEMANS
excerpt, Poems, 1849

BILLY TAYLOR

Little Billy Taylor's
   Gone to be a sailor —
   His ship's for China bound,
Won't the sea perplex him!
   Won't its rolling vex him!
I hope he won't get drowned.

ANON

CASABIANCA

The boy stood on the burning deck
   Whence all but he had fled;
The flame that lit the battle's wreck
   Shone round him o'er the dead.

The flames rolled on. He would not go
   Without his father's word;
That father faint in death below;
   His voice no longer heard.

He called aloud: "Say, father, say
   If yet my task is done!"
He knew not that the chieftain lay
   Unconscious of his son.

"Speak, father!" once again he cried,
   "If I may yet be gone!"
And but the booming shots replied,
   And fast the flames rolled on.

Upon his brow he felt their breath,
   And in his waving hair,
And looked from that lone post of death
   In still yet brave despair;

And shouted but once more aloud,
  "My father! must I stay?"
While o'er him fast through sail and shroud,
  The wreathing fires made way.

They wrapt the ship in splendour wild,
  They caught the flag on high,
And streamed above the gallant child
  Like banners in the sky.

Then came a burst of thunder-sound —
  The boy — oh! where was he?
As of the winds that far around
  With fragments strewed the sea,

With mast, and helm, and pennon fair,
  That well had born their part.
But the noblest thing that perished there
  Was that young faithful heart.

FELICIA HEMANS
Poetical Works, 1836

I saw three ships come sailing by,
  Come sailing by, come sailing by,
I saw three ships come sailing by,
  On New Year's Day in the morning.

And what do you think was in them then,
  Was in them then, was in them then?
And what do you think was in them then,
  On New Year's Day in the morning?

Three pretty girls were in them then,
  Were in them then, were in them then,
Three pretty girls were in them then,
  On New Year's Day in the morning.

One could whistle, and one could sing,
  And one could play on the violin;
Such joy there was at my wedding,
  On New Year's Day in the morning.

ANON

SEA-FEVER

I must go down to the seas again, to the
    lonely sea and the sky,
And all I ask is a tall ship and a star to steer
    her by,
And the wheel's kick and the wind's song
    and the white sails shaking,
And a grey mist on the sea's face and a grey
    dawn breaking.

I must go down to the seas again, for the call
    of the running tide
Is a wild call and a clear call that may not be
    denied;
And all I ask is a windy day with the white
    clouds flying,
And the flung spray and the blown spume,
    and the sea-gulls crying.

I must go down to the seas again, to the
    vagrant gypsy life,
To the gull's way and the whale's way where
    the wind's like a whetted knife;
And all I ask is a merry yarn from a laughing
    fellow-rover,
And quiet sleep and a sweet dream when the
    long trick's over.

JOHN MASEFIELD
Salt-Water Ballads, 1902

THE
DEEP

THE WORLD BELOW
THE BRINE

The world below the brine,
Forests at the bottom of the sea, the
    branches and leaves,
Sea-lettuce, vast lichens, strange flowers and
    seeds, the thick tangle, openings, and
    pink turf,
Different colours, pale grey and green,
    purple, white, and gold, the play of light
    through water,
Dumb swimmers there among the rocks,
    coral, gluten, grass, rushes, and the
    aliment of the swimmers,
Sluggish existences grazing there
    suspended, or slowly crawling close to
    the bottom,
The sperm-whale at the surface blowing air
    and spray, or disporting with his flukes,
The leaden-eyed shark, the walrus, the
    turtle, the hairy sea-leopard, and the
    sting-ray.

Passions there, wars, pursuits, tribes, sight in
    those ocean-depths, breathing that thick-
    breathing air, as so many do,
The change thence to the sight here, and to
    the subtle air breathed by beings like us
    who walk this sphere,
The change onward from ours to that of
    beings who walk other spheres.

WALT WHITMAN
Leaves of Grass, Book XIX:
Seadrift, 1891–2

The horses of the sea
   Rear a foaming crest,
But the horses of the land
   Serve us the best.

The horses of the land
   Munch corn and clover,
While the foaming sea-horses
   Toss and turn over.

CHRISTINA ROSSETTI
Sing Song, 1872

THE MERMAID

I

Who would be
A mermaid fair,
Singing alone,
Combing her hair
Under the sea,
In a golden curl
With a comb of pearl,
On a throne?

II

I would be a mermaid fair;
I would sing to myself the whole of the day,
With a comb of pearl I would comb my hair;
And still as I combed I would sing and say,
"Who is it loves me? who loves not me?"
I would comb my hair till my ringlets would fall,
 Low adown, low adown,
And I should look like a fountain of gold
 Springing alone
 With a shrill inner sound,
 Over the throne
 In the midst of the hall.

ALFRED, LORD TENNYSON
Juvenilia, 1830

THE SANDS OF DEE

"O Mary, go and call the cattle home,
    And call the cattle home,
    And call the cattle home,
    Across the Sands of Dee."
The western wind was wild and dark with foam,
    And all alone went she.

The western tide crept up along the sand,
    And o'er and o'er the sand,
    And round and round the sand,
    As far as eye could see,
The rolling mist came down and hid the land;
    And never home came she.

"Oh! is it weed, or fish, or floating hair —
    A tress of golden hair,
    A drownèd maiden's hair,
    Above the nets at sea?"
Was never salmon yet that shone so fair
    Among the stakes of Dee.

They rowed her in across the rolling foam,
    The cruel, crawling foam,
    The cruel, hungry foam,
  To her grave beside the sea;
But still the boatmen hear her call the cattle home
  Across the Sands of Dee.

CHARLES KINGSLEY

THE LOBSTER

'Tis the voice of the Lobster: I heard him
    declare,
"You have baked me too brown, I must sugar
    my hair."
As a Duck with its eyelids so he with his
    nose
Trims his belt and his buttons and turns out
    his toes.

I passed by his garden and marked, with one
    eye,
How the Owl and the Oyster were sharing a
    pie;
While the Duck and the Dodo, the Lizard
    and Cat,
Were swimming in milk round the brim of a
    hat.

LEWIS CARROLL
Alice's Adventures in Wonderland, 1865

Obillows bounding far,
How wet, how wet ye are!

When first my gaze you met
I said "These waves are wet."

I said it, and am quite
Convinced that I was right.

Who saith that ye are dry?
I give that man the lie.

Thy wetness, O thou sea
Is wonderful to me.

It agitates my heart,
To think how wet thou art.

No object I have met
Is more profoundly wet.

Methinks 'twere vain to try,
O sea, to wipe thee dry.

I therefore will refrain.
Farewell, thou humid main.

A. E. HOUSMAN

FATHER MAPPLE'S HYMN

The ribs and terrors in the whale,
   Arched over me a dismal gloom,
While all God's sun-lit waves rolled by,
   And lift me deepening down to doom.

I saw the opening maw of hell,
   With endless pains and sorrows there;
Which none but they that feel can tell —
   Oh, I was plunging to despair.

In black distress, I called my God,
   When I could scarce believe him mine,
He bowed his ear to my complaints —
   No more the whale did me confine.

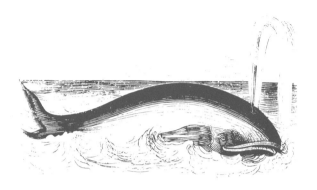

With speed he flew to my relief,
   As on a radiant dolphin borne;
Awful, yet bright, as lightning shone
   The face of my Deliverer God.

My song for ever shall record
   That terrible, that joyful hour;
I give the glory to my God,
   His all the mercy and the power.

HERMAN MELVILLE
Moby–Dick, 1851

ARIEL'S SONG

Full fathom five thy father lies:
  Of his bones are coral made;
Those are pearls that were his eyes:
  Nothing of him that doth fade,
But doth suffer a sea-change
Into something rich and strange.
Sea-nymphs hourly ring his knell:
  Hark! now I hear them, —
    Ding, dong, bell.

WILLIAM SHAKESPEARE
The Tempest, Act I Scene II, 1623

LIKE THE FISH

Like the fish of the bright and twittering fin,
   Bright fish! diving deep as high soars the lark,
So far, far, far, doth the maiden swim,
   Wild song, wild light, in still ocean's dark.

HERMAN MELVILLE
Mardi: And A Voyage Thither, 1849

O sailor, come ashore,
    What have you brought for me?
Red coral, white coral,
    Coral from the sea.

I did not dig it from the ground,
    Nor pluck it from a tree;
Feeble insects made it
    In the stormy sea.

CHRISTINA ROSSETTI
Sing Song, 1872

THE NORTHERN
SEAS

Up! up! let us a voyage take;
　Why sit we here at ease?
Find us a vessel tight and snug
　Bound for the northern seas.

I long to see the northern lights
　With their rushing splendours fly,
Like living things with flaming wings,
　Wide o'er the wondrous sky.

I long to see those icebergs vast
　With heads all crowned with snow,
Whose green roots sleep in the awful deep
　Two hundred fathoms low.

I long to hear the thundering crash
　Of their terrific fall,
And the echoes from a thousand cliffs
　Like lonely voices call.

There shall we see the fierce white bear
　The sleepy seals aground,
And the spouting whales that to and fro
　Sail with a dreary sound.

And while the unsetting sun shines on
　　Through the still heavens' deep blue,
We'll traverse the azure waves, the herds
　　Of the dread sea-horse to view.

We'll pass the shores of solemn pine
　　Where wolves and black bears prowl;
And away to the rocky isles of mist,
　　To rouse the northern fowl.

And there in the wastes of the silent sky
　　With the silent earth below,
We shall see far off to his lonely rock
　　The lonely eagle go.

Then softly, softly will we tread
　　By inland streams, to see
Where the pelican of the silent North
　　Sits there all silently.

MARY HOWITT
Birds & Flowers, 1838

OLD
SALTS

THE OWL AND
THE PUSSYCAT

The Owl and the Pussycat went to sea
  In a beautiful pea-green boat:
They took some honey, and plenty of money
  Wrapped up in a five-pound note.
The Owl looked up to the stars above,
  And sang to a small guitar,
"O lovely Pussy, O Pussy, my love,
  What a beautiful Pussy you are,
    You are,
    You are!
What a beautiful Pussy you are!"

Pussy said to the Owl, "You elegant fowl,
   How charmingly sweet you sing!
Oh! let us be married; too long we have tarried:
   But what shall we do for a ring?"
They sailed away, for a year and a day,
   To the land where the bong-tree grows;
And there in a wood a Piggy-wig stood,
   With a ring at the end of his nose,
      His nose,
      His nose,
   With a ring at the end of his nose.

"Dear Pig, are you willing to sell for one shilling
   Your ring?" Said the Piggy, "I will."
So they took it away, and were married next day
   By the turkey who lives on the hill.
They dined on mince and slices of quince,
   Which they ate with a runcible spoon:
And hand in hand, on the edge of the sand,
   They danced by the light of the moon.
      The moon,
      The moon,
   They danced by the light of the moon.

EDWARD LEAR

COME CHEER UP
MY LADS

Come cheer up my lads, 'tis to glory we steer,
To add something new to this wonderful year;
To honour we call you, not press you like slaves,
For who are so free as the sons of the waves?

> Heart of Oak are our ships, Heart of Oak are our men,
> We always are ready.
> Steady, boys, steady,
> We'll fight and we'll conquer again and again.

We ne'er meet our foes but we wish them to stay,
They never see us but they wish us away;
If they run, why, we follow, and run them ashore,
For if they won't fight us, we cannot do more.

> Heart of Oak are our ships, Heart of Oak are our men,
> We always are ready.
> Steady, boys, steady,
> We'll fight and we'll conquer again and again.

DAVID GARRICK

THE JUMBLIES

They went to sea in a Sieve, they did,
  In a Sieve they went to sea;
In spite of all their friends could say,
On a winter's morn, on a stormy day,
  In a Sieve they went to sea!
And when the Sieve turned round and round,
And everyone cried, "You'll all be drowned!"
They called aloud, "Our Sieve ain't big,
But we don't care a button! We don't care a fig!
  In a Sieve we'll go to sea!"
    Far and few, far and few,
      Are the lands where the Jumblies live;
      Their heads are green, and their hands are blue,
      And they went to sea in a Sieve.

EDWARD LEAR

Three wise men of Gotham,
They went to sea in a bowl,
And if the bowl had been stronger
My song would be longer.

ANON

MISTRESS TOWL

There was an Old Woman named Towl
Who went out to sea with her Owl,
But the Owl was sea-sick
And screamed for physic;
Which sadly annoyed Mistress Towl.

ANON

SIR PATRICK SPENS

The king sits in Dumfermline town
  Drinking the blood-red wine;
"O where will I get a skilful skipper
  To sail this ship of mine?"

Up and spake an elder knight,
  Sat at the king's right knee:
"Sir Patrick Spens is the best sailor
  That ever sailed the sea."

The king has written a broad letter
  And sealed it with his hand.
And sent it to Sir Patrick Spens
  Was walking on the strand.

"To Noroway, to Noroway,
  To Noroway o'er the foam;
The King's own daughter of Noroway,
  'Tis thou must bring her home!"

"Make haste, make haste, my merry men all,
  Our good ship sails the morn."
"Oh say not so, my master dear,
  For I fear a deadly storm."

They had not sailed a league, a league,
   A league, but barely three,
When the sky grew dark, the wind blew loud,
   And angry grew the sea.

The anchor broke, the topmast split,
   'Twas such a deadly storm.
The waves came over the broken ship
   Till all her sides were torn.

O long, long may the ladies sit
   With their fans into their hand,
Or ere they see Sir Patrick Spens
   Come sailing to the strand.

O long, long may the maidens sit
   With their gold combs in their hair,
Before they'll see their own dear loves
   Come home to greet them there.

Half-o'er, half-o'er to Aberdour
   'Tis fifty fathoms deep;
And there lies good Sir Patrick Spens
   With the Scots lords at his feet.

ANON

There was an Old Man in a boat,
Who said, "I'm afloat! I'm afloat!"
When they said, "No! you ain't!" he was
  ready to faint,
That unhappy Old Man in a boat.

EDWARD LEAR
The Book of Nonsense, 1846

PIRATE DITTY

Fifteen men on the Dead Man's Chest —
Yo-ho-ho, and a bottle of rum!
Drink and the devil had done for the rest —
Yo-ho-ho, and a bottle of rum!

ROBERT LOUIS STEVENSON
A Child's Garden of Verses, 1885

When the wind is in the East
'Tis neither good for man nor beast;
When the wind is in the North
The skilful fisher goes not forth;
When the wind is in the South
It blows the bait in the fishes' mouth.
The wind is best when in the West.

ANON

THE SMUGGLER

O my true love's a smuggler and sails
    upon the sea,
And I would I were a seaman to go along
    with he;
To go along with he for the satins and the
    wine,
And run the tubs at Slapton when the stars
    do shine.

The King he is a proud man in his grand red
    coat,
But I do love a smuggler in a little fishing-
    boat;
For he runs the Mallins lace and he spends
    his money free,
And I would I were a seaman to go along
    with he.

ANON

BOBBY SHAFTOE

Bobby Shaftoe's gone to sea,
Silver buckles at his knee;
He'll come back and marry me,
    Bonny Bobby Shaftoe.

Bobby Shaftoe's bright and fair,
Combing down his yellow hair,
He's my love for evermore
    Bonny Bobby Shaftoe.

Bobby Shaftoe's looking out,
All his ribbons fly about,
All the ladies give a shout,
    Hey for Bobby Shaftoe

Bobby Shaftoe's gettin' a bairn
For to dandle in his arm;
In his arm and on his knee,
    Bobby Shaftoe loves me.

ANON

THE FISHERMAN'S SONG

When haddocks leave the Firth of Forth,
And mussels leave the shore,
When oysters climb up Berwick Law,
We'll go to sea no more,
No more,
We'll go to sea no more.

O blithely shines the bonnie sun
Upon the Isle of May,
And blithely rolls the morning tide
Into St. Andrew's bay.

ANON

RIDDLE

Over the water,
And under the water,
And always with its head down.

[Nail on the bottom of a ship]

ANON

I've a lad in Golspie,
I've a lad at sea,
I've a lad in Golspie
And his number is twenty-three.
I can wash a sailor's shirt,
And I can wash it clean;
I can wash a sailor's shirt,
And bleach it on the green.
I can chew tobacco,
I can smoke a pipe,
I can kiss a bonny lad
At ten o'clock at night.

ANON

A tailor, who sailed from Quebec,
In a storm ventured once upon deck;
   But the waves of the sea
   Were as strong as could be
And he tumbled in up to his neck.

ANON

A SMUGGLER'S SONG

If you wake at midnight, and hear a horse's feet,
Don't go drawing back the blind, or looking in the street,
Them that asks no questions isn't told a lie.
Watch the wall, my darling, while the gentlemen go by!
   Five and twenty ponies
   Trotting through the dark —
   Brandy for the Parson,
   'Baccy for the Clerk;
   Laces for a lady, letters for a spy,
And watch the wall, my darling, while the gentlemen go by!

Running round the woodlump if you chance to find
Little barrels, roped and tarred, all full of brandy-wine,
Don't you shout to come and look, nor use 'em for your play.
Put the brushwood back again — and they'll be gone next day!

If you see the stable-door setting open wide;
If you see a tired horse lying down inside;
If your mother mends a coat cut about and tore;
If the lining's wet and warm — don't you ask no more!

If you do as you've been told, likely there's a chance,
You'll be give a dainty doll, all the way from France,
With a cap of Valenciennes, and a velvet hood —
A present from the Gentlemen, along o' being good!
   Five and twenty ponies,
   Trotting through the dark —
   Brandy for the Parson,
   'Baccy for the Clerk.
Them that asks no questions, isn't told a lie —
So watch the wall, my darling, while the Gentlemen go by!

RUDYARD KIPLING

EARLY IN THE MORNING

What shall we do with the drunken sailor,
What shall we do with the drunken sailor,
What shall we do with the drunken sailor,
Early in the morning.

    Hooray and up she rises,
    Hooray and up she rises,
    Hooray and up she rises,
    Early in the morning.

Put him in the longboat until he's sober,
Put him in the longboat until he's sober,
Put him in the longboat until he's sober,
Early in the morning.

    CHORUS: Hooray . . .

Pull out the plug and wet him all over,
Pull out the plug and wet him all over,
Pull out the plug and wet him all over,
Early in the morning.

    CHORUS: Hooray . . .

Put him in the scuppers with a hosepipe on
    him,
Put him in the scuppers with a hosepipe on
    him,
Put him in the scuppers with a hosepipe on
    him,
Early in the morning.

    CHORUS: Hooray . . .

Heave him by the leg in a running bowline,
Heave him by the leg in a running bowline,
Heave him by the leg in a running bowline,
Early in the morning.

    CHORUS: Hooray . . .

Tie him to the taffrail when she's yard-arm
    under,
Tie him to the taffrail when she's yard-arm
    under,
Tie him to the taffrail when she's yard-arm
    under,
Early in the morning.

    CHORUS: Hooray . . .

ANON

SEA
DREAMS

BY THE SEA

Why does the sea moan evermore?
  Shut out from heaven it makes its moan,
It frets against the boundary shore:
All earth's full rivers cannot fill
The sea, that drinking thirsteth still.

Sheer miracles of loveliness
  Lie hid on its unlooked-on bed:
Anemones, salt, passionless,
Blow flower-like — just enough alive
To blow and multiply and thrive.

Shells quaint with curve or spot or spike
  Encrusted live things argus-eyed,
All fair alike yet all unlike,
Are born without a pang, and die
Without a pang, and so pass by.

CHRISTINA ROSSETTI

I SIT UP HERE
AT MIDNIGHT

I sit up here at midnight,
  The wind is in the street,
The rain besieges the windows
  Like the sound of many feet.

I see the street lamps flicker,
  I see them wink and fail,
The streets are wet and empty,
  It blows an easterly gale.

Some think of the fisher skipper
  Beyond the Inchcape stone;
But I of the fisher woman
  That lies at home alone.

She raises herself on her elbow
  And watches the firelit floor;
Her eyes are bright with terror
  Her heart beats fast and sore.

Between the roar of the flurries,
  When the tempest holds his breath
She holds her breathing also —
  It is all as still as death.

She can hear the cinders dropping,
  The cat that purrs in its sleep —
The foolish fisher woman!
  Her heart is on the deep.

ROBERT LOUIS STEVENSON
A Child's Garden of Verses, 1885

A SHIP, AN ISLE,
A SICKLE MOON

A ship, an isle, a sickle moon —
With few but with how splendid stars
The mirrors of the sea are strewn
Between their silver bars!

An isle beside an isle she lay,
The pale ship anchored in the bay,
While in the young moon's port of gold
A star-ship — as the mirrors told —
Put forth its great and lonely light
To the unreflecting Ocean, Night.
And still, a ship upon her seas,
The isle and the island cypresses
Went sailing on without the gale:
And still there moved the moon so pale,
A crescent ship without a sail!

JAMES ELROY FLECKER
Collected Poems, 1916

ANNABEL LEE

It was many and many a year ago,
  In a kingdom by the sea,
That a maiden there lived whom you may know
  By the name of Annabel Lee;
And this maiden she lived with no other thought
  Than to love and be loved by me.

I was a child and she was a child,
  In this kingdom by the sea,
But we loved with a love that was more than love,
  I and my Annabel Lee;
With a love that the winged seraphs of heaven
  Coveted her and me.

And this was the reason that, long ago,
  In this kingdom by the sea,
A wind blew out of a cloud, chilling
  My beautiful Annabel Lee;
So that her highborn kinsmen came
  And bore her away from me,
To shut her up in the sepulchre
  In this kingdom by the sea.

The angels, not half so happy in heaven,
   Went envying her and me;
Yes! that was the reason (as all men know,
   In this kingdom by the sea)
That the wind came out of the cloud by night,
   Chilling and killing my Annabel Lee.

But our love it was stronger by far than the love
   Of those who were older than we,
   Of many far wiser than we;
And neither the angels in heaven above,
   Nor the demons down under the sea,
Can ever dissever my soul from the soul
   Of the beautiful Annabel Lee.

For the moon never beams, without bringing me dreams
   Of the beautiful Annabel Lee;
And the stars never rise, but I see the bright eyes
   Of the beautiful Annabel Lee;
And so, all the night-tide, I lie down by the side
Of my darling — my darling — my life and my bride,
   In her sepulchre there by the sea,
   In her tomb by the sounding sea.

EDGAR ALLAN POE
Works, 1850

THE SEA GYPSY

I am fevered with the sunset,
I am fretful with the bay,
For the wander-thirst is on me
And my soul is in Cathay.

There's a schooner in the offing,
With her topsail shot with fire,
And my heart has gone aboard her
For the Islands of Desire.

I must forth again to-morrow!
With the sunset I must be
Hull down on the trail of rapture
In the wonder of the sea.

RICHARD HOVEY
More Songs From Vagabondia, 1896

ACROSS THE SEA

I walked in the lonesome evening,
   And who so sad as I,
When I saw the young men and maidens
   Merrily passing by?
      To thee, my love, to thee —
      So fain would I come to thee!
While the ripples fold upon sands of gold
   And I look across the sea.

I stretch out my hands; who will clasp them?
   I call — thou repliest no word:
Oh, why should heart-longing be weaker
   Than the waving wings of a bird!
     To thee my love, to thee —
     So fain would I come to thee!
For the tide's at rest from east to west,
   And I look across the sea.

There's joy in the hopeful morning,
   There's peace in the parting day,
There's sorrow with every lover
   Whose true-love is far away.
     To thee, my love, to thee —
     So fain would I come to thee!
And the water's bright in a still moonlight,
   As I look across the sea.

WILLIAM ALLINGHAM
Fifty Modern Poems, 1865

O CAPTAIN!
MY CAPTAIN!

O Captain! my Captain! our fearful trip is done,
The ship has weathered every ruck, the prize
　　we sought is won,
The port is near, the bells I hear, the people
　　all exulting,
While follow eyes the steady keel, the vessel
　　grim and daring;
　But O heart! heart! heart!
　　O the bleeding drops of red!
　　　Where on the deck my Captain lies,
　　　Fallen cold and dead.

O Captain! my Captain! rise up and hear the bells;
Rise up — for you the flag is flung — for you
    the bugle trills,
For you bouquets and ribban'd wreaths —
    for you the shores crowding,
For they call, the swaying mass, their eager
    faces turning;
  Here, Captain! dear father!
    This arm beneath your head!
      It is some dream that on the deck
        You've fallen cold and dead.

My Captain does not answer, his lips are
    pale and still,
My father does not feel my arm, he has no
    pulse nor will;
The ship is anchor'd safe and sound, its
    voyage closed and done,
From fearful trip the victor ship comes in
    with object won;
  Exult, O shores! and sing, O bells!
    But I with mournful tread,
      Walk the deck my Captain lies,
      Fallen cold and dead.

WALT WHITMAN

Leaves of Grass, Book XVII:
Memories of President Lincoln, 1891 – 2

ECHOES

The full sea rolls and thunders
   In glory and in glee.
O, bury me not in the senseless earth
   But in the living sea!

Ay, bury me where it surges
   A thousand miles from shore,
And in its brotherly unrest
   I'll range for evermore.

WILLIAM ERNEST HENLEY
excerpt, Poems, 1912

SPIRIT OF FREEDOM, THOU DOST LOVE THE SEA

Spirit of freedom, thou dost love the sea,
Trackless and storm-tost ocean wild and free,
Faint symbol of thine own eternity.
  The seagulls wheel and soar and fearless roam,
  The storm petrel dashes through the foam;
The mighty billows heave, the tempests roar,
The diapason thunders shake the shore
And chant the song of freedom evermore.

HENRY NEHEMIAH DODGE
Christus Victor: A Student's Reverie CXIX, 1899

SWEET AND LOW

Sweet and low, sweet and low,
  Wind of the western sea,
Low, low, breathe and blow,
  Wind of the western sea!
  Over the rolling waters go,
  Come from the dying moon, and blow,
  Blow him again to me;
While my little one, while my pretty one, sleeps.

Sleep and rest, sleep and rest,
  Father will come to thee soon;
Rest, rest, on mother's breast,
  Father will come to thee soon;
  Father will come to this babe in the nest
  Silver sails all out of the west
  Under the silver moon;
Sleep, my little one, sleep, my pretty one, sleep.

ALFRED, LORD TENNYSON
The Princess, A Medley, 1850

CROSSING THE BAR

Sunset and evening star,
  And one clear call for me!
And may there be no moaning of the bar,
  When I put out to sea,

But such a tide as moving seems asleep,
  Too full for sound and foam,
When that which drew from out the
    boundless deep
  Turns again home.

Twilight and evening bell,
  And after that the dark!
And may there be no sadness of farewell,
  When I embark;

For tho' from out our bourne of Time and Place
  The flood may bear me far,
I hope to see my Pilot face to face
  When I have crost the bar.

ALFRED, LORD TENNYSON

THE SECRET
OF THE SEA

Ah! what pleasant visions haunt me
 As I gaze upon the sea!
All the old romantic legends,
 All my dreams, come back to me.

Most of all, the Spanish ballad
 Haunts me oft, and tarries long,
Of the noble Count Arnaldos
 And the sailor's mystic song.

Telling how the Count Arnaldos,
 With his hawk upon his hand,
Saw a fair and stately galley,
 Steering onward to the land; —

How he heard the ancient helmsman
 Chant a song so wild and clear,
That the sailing sea-bird slowly
 Poised upon the mast to hear,

Till his soul was full of longing,
    And he cried, with impulse strong, —
"Helmsman! for the love of heaven,
    Teach me, too, that wondrous song!"

"Wouldst thou," so the helmsman answered,
    "Learn the secret of the sea,
Only those who brave its dangers
    Comprehend its mystery!"

In each sail that skims the horizon,
    In each landward-blowing breeze,
I behold that stately galley,
    Hear those mournful melodies;

Till my soul is full of longing
    For the secret of the sea,
And the heart of the great ocean
    Sends a thrilling pulse through me.

HENRY WADSWORTH LONGFELLOW
Complete Poetical Works, 1864

WHAT ARE HEAVY?

What are heavy? Sea-sand and sorrow;
What are brief? Today and tomorrow;
What are frail? Spring blossoms and youth;
What are deep? The ocean and truth.

CHRISTINA ROSSETTI
Sing Song, 1872

THE POETS

ALLINGHAM, William
(1824–1889) Ireland
Born in Ballyshannon in Donegal, Allingham
spent most of his life working as a customs
officer. His great love for the literature and the
peasantry of his native land inspired him to
write.

BEDDOES, Thomas Lovell
(1803–1849) UK
A studious, melancholy man, Beddoes studied
medicine and spent most of his short adult life in
Zürich, Switzerland. He is best remembered for
the often lyrical, sometimes macabre *Death's
Jest-Book* (1850), published after his suicide.

BRIDGES, Robert
(1844–1930) UK
Bridges' best-known works were published in
Shorter Poems (1873–1893) and *Poetical Works*
(1898–1905). Of the longer works, *Demeter*
(1905) and the remarkable *The Testament of
Beauty* (1929) are notable. He was appointed
poet laureate in 1913.

BYRON, George Gordon, Lord (6th Baron of
Rochdale)
(1788–1824) UK
Byron, perhaps the greatest figure of the
Romantic age, inherited his title at ten. In a life
filled with love affairs and scandals, Byron
traveled throughout Europe, but found time to
write many narrative poems, including *Childe
Harold* (1812–1818) and many lyrics and
dramas. In 1824, he set out to give his support to
the Greek rebels. He died of a fever at
Missolonghi.

CARROLL, Lewis (Charles Lutwidge Dodgson)
(1832–1898) UK
Lewis Carroll rapidly became famous for his two
great works of fantasy and distorted logic, *Alice's
Adventures in Wonderland* (1865) and *Through
the Looking-glass* (1872), but he was already
celebrated in academic circles as a lecturer in
mathematics at Oxford. Queen Victoria,

expressing her admiration for *Alice*, asked
Carroll for a copy of his next book and was
dismayed to receive a learned tome about
Euclidian geometry.

CLOUGH, Arthur Hugh
(1819–1861) UK
A scholar, poet, and wit, Clough is remembered
chiefly for the *New Decalogue*, a skeptical version
of the Ten Commandments, and the famous "Say
not the struggle naught availeth."

COOPER, James Fenimore
(1789–1851) USA
Expelled from Yale, Cooper had an adventurous
youth, living in a pioneer settlement, then
working as a sailor. He wrote many popular
novels, including *The Spy* (1821), *The Pathfinder*
(1840), *The Deerslayer* (1841), and of course *The
Last of the Mohicans* (1826), an account of the
North American Indian Wars.

DAVY, Sir Humphry
(1778–1829) UK
Davy was a professor of chemistry at the Royal
Institution. He invented the miner's safety lamp
which still bears his name. His collected prose
and verse were published in 1840.

DICKINSON, Emily Elizabeth
(1830–1886) USA
The daughter of a wealthy lawyer from Amherst,
Massachusetts, Emily Dickinson lived the quiet
life of a respectable intellectual. She had several
very intelligent male friends, but was otherwise a
recluse for the last twenty-five years of her life.
No one knew until she died that she had written
more than a thousand poems of remarkable
sensitivity and originality. Dickinson expressed
the sharp, ecstatic pangs occasioned by everyday
things precisely observed. Her images were
eccentric, witty, and concise.

FLECKER, James Elroy
(1884–1915) UK
A prodigious and skillful poet whose imagery is
often too rich for modern taste, Flecker is
principally remembered for *The Golden Journey*

to *Samarkand* (1913) and *Hassan* (1922), an opulent verse drama.

GARRICK, David

(1717–1779) UK
The greatest actor of the eighteenth century is commemorated by the London club and the West End theater that bear his name. Garrick's literary reputation rests largely on his letters and the comedy *The Clandestine Marriage* (1766), written in collaboration with George Colman.

HEMANS, Felicia Dorothea

(1793–1835) UK
A very popular poet during her lifetime, Felicia Hemans' work is frequently stirring and heroic, and was a favorite choice for recitations. Among her best-known poems are "Casabianca" and "The Homes of England."

HENLEY, William Ernest

(1849–1903) UK
Henley was a critic, dramatist, anthologist, editor, and poet. Lame from early youth, Henley was a curious amalgam of kindness and irascibility. A close friend of Robert Louis Stevenson, Henley's life was marked by the courage with which he faced his misfortunes expressed most memorably in "Invictus." His collected works appeared in 1908.

HOUSMAN, Alfred Edward

(1859–1936) UK
A poet and classical scholar, Housman was a Professor of Latin at University College, London, and later at Cambridge. He is best remembered for *A Shropshire Lad* (1896), a collection of pastoral lyrics which are strongly influenced by traditional English ballads and classical verse. His later work, collected in *Last Poems* (1922) and *More Poems* (published posthumously in 1936), has a more imaginative, modern feel.

HOVEY, Richard

(1864–1900) USA
After trying his hand at painting, the priesthood, and newspaper work, Hovey journeyed through Nova Scotia and New Brunswick with Bliss Carman, publishing *Songs from Vagabondia*

(1894). His best-known poems include "Men of Dartmouth" and "Stein Song."

HOWITT, Mary (née Botham)

(1799–1888) UK
Wife of author William Howitt and mother of twelve children, Mary Howitt, a Quaker, collaborated with her husband and published more than a hundred books in her own right. Among other claims to fame, she was the first English translator of Hans Christian Andersen.

KINGSLEY, Charles

(1819–1875) UK
Born in England at Holne, Dartmoor, Kingsley became rector of Eversley in Hampshire (1844) after a Cambridge education. A novelist, journalist, and historian, he was Professor of Modern History at Cambridge from 1860 to 1869.

KIPLING, (Joseph) Rudyard

(1865–1936) UK
Born in Bombay and educated in England, Kipling returned to India in 1882 and rapidly acquired a reputation as a brilliant reporter and satirical poet. He settled in London in 1889. His most popular works include *The Jungle Books* (1894–5), *Stalky and Co.* (1899), *Kim* (1901), and *Just So Stories* (1902). He was a fine wordsmith; "A word," he said, "should fall in its place like a bell in a full chime."

LANDOR, Walter Savage

(1775–1864) UK
Apart from collections of verse such as *Gebir* (1798) and *The Hellenics* (1846–7), Landor also published many popular lyrics such as "Ianthe Dirce" and, perhaps most famous, "Rose Aylmer." Forced to leave Oxford because of his views, he spent much of his life in Italy.

LEAR, Edward

(1812–1888) UK
Principally known as the father of nonsense verse and chief exponent of the limerick, Lear was also a considerable traveler and so fine a painter that he was invited to teach Queen Victoria to paint in watercolors. His *Book of*

Nonsense (1846) was written for the grand-children of his patron, the Earl of Derby.

LONGFELLOW, Henry Wadsworth
(1807–1882) USA

A professor of modern languages at Bowdoin College and Harvard University, Longfellow traveled widely and wrote prolifically. His best-known works include *Ballads and Other Poems* (1841), which contains "The Wreck of the Hesperus"; *The Song of Hiawatha* (1855); and *Tales of a Wayside Inn* (1863), which features the famous "Paul Revere's Ride."

MASEFIELD, John
(1878–1967) UK

A poet and novelist, author of two children's classic novels, *The Midnight Folk* (1927), and *A Box of Delights* (1935). His best-known poems are "Sea-Fever" and "Reynard the Fox" (1919).

MELVILLE, Herman
(1819–1891) USA

Born in New York, Melville had perhaps the most adventurous life of all the modern writers. A sailor, he served on the whaler *Dolly* and, in 1842, having rounded Cape Horn, abandoned his ship and its brutal captain and sought refuge in the Marquesas Islands. Here he and his friend were held captive by the cannibal tribe, the Typees. He recounted this tale in *Typee: A Peep at Polynesian Life* (1846). His greatest book, however, is the tale of Captain Ahab's obsessive hunt of the great white whale in *Moby Dick* (1851).

NEWBOLT, Sir Henry
(1862–1938) UK

Newbolt, a patriotic and heroic poet, is known for his stirring verses which lend themselves readily to recitation, including "The Fighting Téméraire" (1897), "Admirals All" (1897), "Drake's Drum" (1914), and most famously "Vitaï Lampada," which begins "There's a breathless hush in the Close tonight/Ten to make and the match to win . . ."

POE, Edgar Allan
(1809–1849) USA

Master of the macabre, Poe was born in Boston, Massachusetts, and educated in England. Although "The Raven" (1845), "Annabel Lee" (1849), and "The Bells" (1849) are well loved, Poe will always be principally remembered for his haunting and resonant tales of horror such as "The Murders in the Rue Morgue" (1841), "The Pit and the Pendulum" (1842), and "The Tell-Tale Heart" (1843).

ROSSETTI, Christina Georgina
(1830–1894) UK

Sister of the poet and painter Dante Gabriel Rossetti, Christina led a sad life and failed to fulfill her early exceptional promise. She twice rejected suitors because of her high Anglican religious principles, and her verses are devout and full of the sadness of "what might have been." Her first collection, *Goblin Market* (1862), is her finest, but *Sing-Song* (1872) is full of charming, simple verses for children. She was always frail and, at the time of *Sing-Song*'s composition, was very close to death from Grave's disease. Thereafter she taught with her mother and wrote "morally improving" verse.

SCOTT, Sir Walter
(1771–1832) UK

A barrister, novelist, and balladeer, Scott collected the ballads of his native Border country in *Minstrelsy of the Scottish Border* (1802–3). Two years later he produced his first original verse romance, *The Lay of the Last Minstrel* (1805), then *Marmion* (1808). He then devoted himself to writing novels, including *Waverley* (1814), *Rob Roy* (1818), *The Heart of Midlothian* (1818), *Ivanhoe* (1820), and many many others. Ruined by the downfall of his partner, James Ballantyne, and his publisher Constable, he devoted years of unceasing effort to paying off his creditors. This was only achieved after his death, when his hundreds of copyrights were sold.

SHAKESPEARE, William
(1564–1616) UK
Shakespeare merits every one of the superlatives devoted to him. Born and educated in Stratford-on-Avon, Warwickshire, he moved to London to be an actor. Shakespeare then rapidly proved himself to be the most versatile, perceptive, and expressive poet, dramatist, and chronicler of human foibles and aspirations the world has ever seen.

STEVENSON, Robert Louis
(1850–1894) UK
Stevenson was a master stylist and supremely imaginative writer who contrived to lead a hero's life despite often crippling illness. All his life he suffered from chronic bronchial problems and acute nervous excitability. He nonetheless traveled extensively, wrote many fine essays and novels, and in *A Child's Garden of Verses* (1885) applied his highly developed gifts of imagination and sympathy to the emotions and enthusiasms of childhood. In so doing he can be said to have invented a whole new genre of verse. In 1888 he traveled in the South Seas and at last settled with his family in Samoa, where the natives called him "Tusitala" (the tale-teller). He died there of a brain hemorrhage. His novels include *Treasure Island* (1883), *Kidnapped* (1886), *Catriona* (1893), and, for older readers, *The Strange Case of Dr. Jekyll and Mr. Hyde* (1886).

TENNYSON, Alfred, Lord
(1809–1892) UK
Although the most honored and fêted poet of the Victorian era, Tennyson liked to live "far from the madding crowd" in Hampshire or on the Isle of Wight. He was very prolific and, although he never wrote specifically for children, many of his works have become firm favorites with young people because of their grand romantic subject matter or because they are ideal for reciting.

THOMPSON, D'Arcy Wentworth
(1829–1902) UK
Thompson was a Classics Master at Edinburgh University, where his pupils included Robert Louis Stevenson. He wrote *Nursery Nonsense or Rhymes without Reason* (1864) for his small son.

WHITMAN, Walt
(1819–1892) USA
Initially a printer and only an occasional writer, Whitman seemed set for a successful career as an editor, but his political integrity hindered him and he found himself earning a living as a carpenter and builder until he published the startlingly original *Leaves of Grass* in 1855. At first ill-received, it slowly grew in popularity until his then employer — the government — became aware of its lowly clerk's part-time job and dismissed him on the grounds of the book's "immorality." This caused a furor which at once sold many copies of the book and helped establish Whitman's enormous reputation.

WORDSWORTH, William
(1770–1850) UK
The poet laureate lived in Grasmere in the English Lake District with his sister Dorothy. At his best, as in "The Prelude" or "Tintern Abbey," Wordsworth was a brilliant, thoughtful nature poet; at his worst he was capable of gaucheness and banality.

THE PAINTERS

page

Title	William Marshall Brown (1863–1936)	56	Carl Bille (1815–1898)
6	Alexander M. Rossi (fl. 1870–1903)	60	Oswald Achanbach (1827–1905)
10	Thomas James Lloyd (1849–1910)	64	David James (fl. 1881–1895)
12	Frants Peder Diderik (1850–1908)	68	William Lionel Wyllie (1851–1931)
16	Peter Christian Dommerson (nineteenth century)	78	Hector Caffieri (1847–1932)
		82	Frederick Morgan (1856–1927)
20	Peter Christian Dommerson (nineteenth century)	87	George Chambers (1803–1840)
		95	Sir John Pettie (1839–1893)
24	Creswick Boydell (1889–1894)	98	Edith Hume (fl. 1862–1892)
28	William Marshall Brown (1863–1936)	102	Arthur Gilbert (1819–1895)
30	Robert Clouston Young (1860–1929)	106	Joseph Farquarson (1847–1935)
34	Captain Richard Beechey (1808–1895)	109	Alfred J. Warne Browne (fl. ca. 1884)
38	William Marshall Brown (1863–1936)	113	John MacWhirter RA (1839–1911)
42	George Henry Andrews (1816–1898)	116	Walter C. Hutton (nineteenth/twentieth century)
43	George Balmer (ca. 1806–1846)		
45	James Wilson Carmichael (1800–1868)	120	Erskine Nichol (1825–1904)
48	Joseph Mallord William Turner (1775–1851)	125	George Goodwin Kilburne (1839–1924)
		127	E. Beshays (nineteenth century)
52	Georges Jean-Marie Hacquette (1854–1906)	130	Arthur Gilbert (1819–1895)
		Endpapers	William Langley (nineteenth century/twentieth century)

ACKNOWLEDGMENTS

The art for this book consists of full-color reproductions of oil paintings from the Edwardian and Victorian eras, as well as prints of black-and-white engravings from the same period.

All color pictures are courtesy of the Fine Art Photographic Library, London, except the following:
George Henry Andrews (1816–1898) "Storm in the North Sea with Smack & Barque" on page 42, and George Balmer (ca.1806–1846) "Coast Scene" on page 43, by courtesy of the Board of Trustees of the Victoria & Albert Museum, London/Bridgeman Art Library.

James Wilson Carmichael (1800–1868) "A Dutch Brig on a Port Reach" on page 45 and Carl Bille (1815–1898) "Shipping in Moonlight Waters" on page 120, Bonhams, London/Bridgeman Art Library.

The black-and-white illustration on page 50 is reproduced by courtesy of the Mansell Collection, Ltd. Pages 66 and 67 courtesy of Mary Evans Picture Library.

The poem "I started early, took my dog..." by Emily Dickinson on page 28 is reprinted by permission of the publishers and the Trustees of Amherst College from THE POEMS OF EMILY DICKINSON, Thomas H. Johnson, ed., Cambridge, Mass.: The Belknap Press of Harvard University Press, Copyright 1951, © 1955, 1979, 1983 by the President and Fellows of Harvard College. The poem "Sea-Fever" by John Masefield on page 58 is reprinted by permission of the Society of Authors as the literary representatives of the Estate of John Masefield.

INDEX OF FIRST LINES

A sailor went to sea 27

A ship, an isle, a sickle
moon — 112

A tailor, who sailed from
Quebec, 101

Above the quiet dock at
midnight, 9

Ah! what pleasant visions
haunt me 128

Bobby Shaftoe's gone to sea, 97

But I have sinuous shells, of
pearly hue 71

Come cheer up my lads,
'tis to glory we steer, 86

Dance to your daddy, 20

Fifteen men on the Dead
Man's Chest — 93

Full fathom five thy father
lies: 76

Gathering up the pebbles, 12

Granny and I with dear
Dadu 22

He that has sail'd upon the
dark blue sea, 32

Hey, dorolot, dorolot! 26

Ho! merrily ho! we paddlers
sail! 46

I am fevered with the
sunset, 116

I must go down to the seas
again, 58

I saw three ships come
sailing by, 57

I sit up here at midnight, 110

I started early, took my dog, 28

I walked in the lonesome
evening, 118

If you wake at midnight,
and hear a horse's feet, 102

It is a beauteous evening,
calm and free; 16

It was eight bells ringing, 49

It was many and many a
year ago, 114

I've a lad in Golspie, 100

Last summer time I went to
Dover by the sea, 26

Lightly row, lightly row! 38

Like the fish of the bright
and twittering fin, 77

Little Billy Taylor's 53

Minnie and Winnie 25

My brigantine! 33

O billows bounding far, 73

O Captain! my Captain!
our fearful trip is done, 120

O Mary, go and call the
cattle home, 68

O my true love's a smuggler
and sails upon the sea, 96

O sailor, come ashore, 79

O to sail in a ship! 43

O'er the rippling ocean 34

Oh the white seagull, the
wild seagull, 18

Over the water, 100

Spirit of freedom, thou dost
love the sea, 123

Sunset and evening star, 126

Sweet and low, sweet and
low, 124

Tell me your secrets, pretty
shell, 15

The boy stood on the
burning deck 54

The breaking waves dashed
high, 50

The cliff-top has a carpet 11

The full sea rolls and
thunders 122

The horses of the sea 64

The king sits in Dumfermline
town 90

The Owl and the Pussycat
went to sea 84

The ribs and terrors in the
whale, 74

The tide rises, the tide falls, 19

The world below the brine, 62

There was an Old Man in a
boat, 92

There was an Old Woman
named Towl 89

They went to sea in a Sieve,
they did, 88

Three wise men of Gotham, 89

'Tis the voice of the Lobster:
I heard him declare, 70

To sea! to sea! the calm is o'er 8

Up! up! Let us a voyage
take; 80

Upon the gale she stooped
her side, 42

We built a ship upon the
stairs 23

What are heavy? Sea-sand
and sorrow; 131

What shall we do with the
drunken sailor, 104

When haddocks leave the
Firth of Forth, 98

When I was down beside
the sea 14

When the cabin port-holes
are dark and green 47

When the wind is in the
East 94

Where lies the land to which
the ship would go? 36

Who would be a mermaid
fair, 66

Why does the sea moan
evermore? 108

With ships the sea was
sprinkled far and nigh, 44

Yes, we did a heap o' riggin' 40